Detective

Charlie "Sir" Ringo:

The Case Of The

Brotherhood

of Outlaws

DETECTIVE CHARLIE "SIR" RINGO:

THE CASE OF THE BROTHERHOOD OF OUTLAWS

Hideout Kids Book 8

by

Mike Gleason

Illustrated by Victoria Taylor

FARM STREET PUBLISHING

First published 2019 by Farm Street Publishing
www.hideoutkidsbooks.com

Paperback ISBN 978-1-912207-20-6
Hardback ISBN 978-1-912207-21-3

A CIP catalogue record for this book is available from
the British Library.

Design and typesetting by Head & Heart

To Michelle and Luke,
who inspired me to write these stories
of the Wild West.

TUFF

SADIE

CONTENTS

Dear Reader,

Detective Charlie "Sir" Ringo: The Case of the Brotherhood of Outlaws is the eighth in the series of Hideout Kids books.

After the American Civil War travel in the United States by foot, horse and wagon gave way to travel by steam train. Iron train tracks were laid from the big cities of the East Coast through the Great Plains, across the Rocky Mountains and down into the western states on the Pacific Coast.

Soon tracks and rail routes criss-crossed America. Everybody and everything traveled by rail, including all the gold bars, silver bars and money needed to keep the great country growing.

Criminals and outlaws discovered they could stop and rob the lightly guarded trains. The first train robbery happened in Indiana, carried out by a gang of four brothers named John, William, Simon and Frank Reno. They called themselves the "Brotherhood of Outlaws." They bragged about their success and claimed they "invented" train robbery. To stop The Reno Gang, the United States government called in the powerful Pinkerton Detective Agency.

In this story, the hideout kid Charlie "Sir" Ringo is given his first job as a detective for the Agency. The powerful and good witch Judge June Beak is asked by Pinkerton to send Sheriff Tuff Brunson and Deputy Sadie Marcus to help Charlie arrest John Reno, the leader of the gang.

If you want to curl up with a good story, start curling and turn the page.

Mike Gleason

DETECTIVE CHARLIE "SIR" RINGO:

THE CASE OF THE BROTHERHOOD OF OUTLAWS

CHAPTER ONE

FISH OUT OF WATER

One cloudy June morning, cool summer breezes drifted over the Wild West Texas town of Muleshoe. Ten-year-old Sheriff Tuff Brunson joined Deputy Sadie Marcus and the hungry hideout kids for breakfast in the Happy Days Saloon. They merrily sang Wandering Wanda's favorite song, "Mammas, Don't Let Your Babies Grow Up To Be Cowboys", as they munched on buffalo sausages and fresh duck eggs.

1

After filling their tummies Tuff and Sadie left for the jailhouse.

The soft snores of jailhouse guard Deputy Dan Pigeon could be heard over the steady *buzz* of the cicadas perched in the bright green trees around the town. As usual, Deputy Dan was sound asleep when he was supposed to guard the jail. "Time to wake up, Deputy," Tuff ordered as he stepped through the door. "You're off night duty." He shook Deputy Dan's shoulders.

"Huh?" Deputy Dan groaned as he sat up. "Did you say 'It's time for breakfast?' I smell sausages."

"No, I didn't. How is the prisoner? Any trouble?"

"The prisoner is happy, Sheriff," said the vicious outlaw Sam Bass from inside his cell. "Today I'm leavin' this jail."

"You're wrong, Sam," Tuff said. "You are not leaving for a long time."

"Crime doesn't pay," Sadie said.

"You'll see, you pimply deputy," Sam said to Sadie. "My army of pets is on the way. They're gonna get me out."

"Your pets?" Tuff laughed as he and Sadie walked into the jail's office. "C'mon Sadie, let's play a quick game of 'Go Fish'. This outlaw isn't going anywhere."

"LOOK OUT FOR THESE CREATURES!" someone yelled outside.

"Who's that?" Sadie asked. "It sounds like Howard the Coward."

"Tuff, Sadie, come quick! Muleshoe is under attack."

Tuff and Sadie burst out of the jailhouse office.

"What the –?" Tuff exclaimed.

Hundreds of lizards jumped out of the sandy ground and scampered around Muleshoe.

"Run," Howard the Coward warned. "Get inside the buildings and lock the doors."

Tuff grabbed one of the lizards by the

tail and took a good look at it. Its long skinny caramel body had smooth scales with black cross bands. Heavy eyelids covered its beady eyes.

"Wait," Tuff said. "There's nothing to worry about. These lizards are called skinks. They only eat insects. They won't bite any of

the children. It's just another trick from that smelly Sam Bass. I'll deal with him now."

He carried the lizard into the jailhouse. Sadie followed him.

"Ha," Sam said from behind the jail bars. "I see my skinks arrived. My henchman Laughing Larry snuck up to Muleshoe and let 'em loose. I told you I was gettin' out today. You don't have enough bullwhips in the world to tame them, Sheriff. They're takin' over the town."

"You make me laugh. I know all about these little creatures," Tuff said. He tossed the skink on the floor. "These skinks are also called 'sandfish'. They burrow through the sand, just like fish swim through water. Since you look like a slimy fish that must be why you like them."

"That's right, Sheriff," Sam said. "I thought how I could escape. I told 'em to burrow a tunnel under the jail and get me out. I think I hear 'em scratchin' now!"

"SCRATCH! SCRATCH!"

Sam stared down at the dirt floor of his jail cell. A mound of dirt grew bigger as the furious sound of digging got louder.

A head broke through the floor. "What's up, genius?" snarled Wild Thing, Judge June's pet pink fairy armadillo. "Thanks for inviting your pet lizards to town. You know what my favorite snack is?"

"Oh, no, it's you," Sam said. "What is your favorite snack?"

"Reptiles," growled Wild Thing. "And my favorite reptile is a skink. Bring 'em on. I've invited my friends too. We like a change from the cockroach diet. Skinks are like ice cream for us."

Tuff and Sadie heard a ruckus and looked outside. A fez of armadillos thundered into town. Wild Thing joined her friends as they burrowed under the ground to chase the skinks, which were in a hurry to escape the armadillos' hungry jaws.

"It's an underground feeding frenzy." Tuff laughed. Soon the skinks were gone and the peaceful morning returned to Muleshoe.

"Hey Sam, try not to think." Tuff smiled at Sam Bass, who sat in his jail cell, his head in his hands. "It won't do you any good."

"Let's go find Judge June," Sadie said. "Maybe she'll have a job for us."

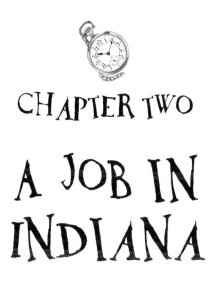

CHAPTER TWO

A JOB IN INDIANA

"I bet she's in the Happy Days Saloon," Tuff said.

"Nope, I'm right behind you," the good witch Judge Junia "June" Beak said quietly.

Tuff and Sadie almost jumped out of their boots.

"Gosh you really scared us, sneaking up behind like that," Sadie said.

"Sorry guys," Judge June said. She held a

piece of parchment with the word **URGENT** written across the top. "I've been looking for you. I saw Wild Thing gobbling those skinks. I bet she will be a bit fat when she comes home. She'll probably sleep all day."

"Isn't that what she always does?" Sadie asked. "Wait, there she is now."

The kids giggled as they saw Wandering Wanda roll the super-stuffed Wild Thing along the ground. "My little hangrydillo girlfriend can't even walk." Wandering Wanda laughed. "Maybe I'll roll her under a tree so she can sleep."

"I can't walk but I can still toot," Wild Thing growled. "How about this doozy? Bet it stinks like skinks."

"TOOT!"

"That's horrible Wild Thing." Judge June coughed as they all covered their noses.

"Tuff and Sadie, come with me to the hut," she said. "I need to send you on a job right away."

Tuff and Sadie followed Judge June through the hut's bright yellow door. Tuff felt the cool breeze as they closed the door behind them. In one corner a giant stuffed black bear glared out with his yellow eyes, sharp teeth and claws.

Wait, did his leg just move? Tuff wondered.

Judge June's familiar, Hooter the Owl, was perched on his stool in another corner.

"Good morning, Tuff and Sadie," Hooter cooed as he licked his beak with his long gray tongue. "Those skinks are delicious. I joined Wild Thing and tasted a few. I hope Sam invites them back again soon." A bit of liquid trickled down his chest.

"Yuck!" Sadie said.

"Don't worry, Sadie," Hooter hooted. "It's just lizard juice."

"Please listen carefully," Judge June said as she sat at her table with the parchment in front of her. "I've had a telegram from Pinkerton Detective Agency. They have hired your friend, the hideout kid Charlie "Sir" Ringo. The agency calls him the 'Cowboy Detective'. Charlie wants to help solve crimes, instead of working as a cowboy."

"That's great," Tuff said. "I always thought Charlie would make a good detective. Pinkerton Agency is the best in the world. How did he get the job?"

Judge June replied, "Pinkerton wanted somebody different – a kid cowboy – who outlaws would not think is a detective. Also, they know I'll give him magical powers to help with his work. Don't forget he's only ten years old, like you."

"Is Charlie on a job already?" Sadie asked.

"Yes," Judge June said, "a very difficult job. Pinkerton sent him to find John Reno, head of The Reno Gang. He's the most wanted outlaw in the United States."

"The Reno Gang," Tuff exclaimed. "I read about them in the magazine *This Week in the Wild West*. Four teenage brothers named

John, Frank, William and Simon. They claim to have 'invented' train robbery. They call themselves the 'Brotherhood of Outlaws.'"

"Exactly," Judge June said. "They were the first outlaws to rob a train. They also hold up banks and county treasury offices. Where there's money, they try to steal it."

"Has Charlie found them?" asked Sadie.

"Yes," Judge June answered. "Charlie's motto is, 'Don't chase your tail.' So Charlie went straight to Hoosier, in the State of Indiana, where The Reno Gang grew up. Sure enough he found them there, hiding in plain sight. All the other residents have left Hoosier. Only the brothers live there now."

"If it's Charlie's first big case," Sadie said, "I bet he's excited. And probably nervous."

"Pinkerton needs our help," Judge June said. "Charlie can't bring in The Reno Gang on his own so he needs to capture their leader first. Trouble is John's brothers are always with him."

"Anybody else to worry about?" Tuff asked.

"Yes. The honest people of Indiana want to take the law into their own hands. John Reno is the most hated man in the state. They'll hurt the gang's ringleader if they get their hands on him," Judge June said.

"What can we do to help Charlie?" Tuff asked as his hand dropped to the sturdy handle of his whip.

"What I'd like you to do is this," Judge June continued. "There is a US Army prison just across the Indiana state border. It's near St. Louis, Missouri. Remember, you and Sadie passed through St. Louis on your way out west."

"Of course," Sadie said. "Where the test elephant crossed the Mississippi River bridge."

"I want you to join Charlie, arrest John Reno and get him to that prison," Judge June said. "If you can, his brothers will likely follow him and try to set him free. With any luck, the Army will then be able to capture them and throw the whole gang in prison."

"We're ready," Tuff and Sadie said.

"Good. Indiana is too far to ride so you must go to The Cave with your horses."

Tuff said, "We haven't been to The Cave since we went back in time to rescue Jedediah Smith from Chief Black Bear and the grizzlies."

"And we haven't seen Spiky for ages," Sadie said.

"The Cave can also help you travel into the future and great distances in the present. Spiky the Cactus will send you to Indiana in no time. His password is 'Doom'. Now close your eyes tightly," Judge June said.

Tuff felt the cool breeze as he heard Judge June chant the spell that would help them on their mission.

"You may open your eyes now," the magical witch said. She gazed at them with her almond-shaped blue-gray eyes. "Remember my most important rule. It's easier to *stay* out of trouble than to *get* out. Be very careful. Oh, one more thing. Charlie should have a sidekick helping him. Once you finish your job, bring them both back to Muleshoe. I'd like to see them."

CHAPTER THREE

WELCOME TO HOOSIER

Tuff and Sadie dashed through the door of Judge June's den. Just outside was the fattest pink fairy armadillo they had ever seen, followed close behind by a giggling Wandering Wanda. Wild Thing looked like a giant pink balloon.

"You look even fatter." Tuff laughed at Wild Thing. "If I stuck a needle in you I bet you'd explode and cover Muleshoe with chewed-up skinks!"

"BURP," was all Wild Thing could say.

"Ha," Sadie said. "She's so fat she can't talk. Her lips are almost swollen shut."

"Don't make fun of me," Wild Thing growled with a tiny voice through her puffy lips. "Or you'll be sorry."

"Yeah right," Tuff said. "C'mon, Sadie. Let's get out of pink balloon's way. It will probably take her all day to get to her bed."

Wandering Wanda said, "I'll help the little gal. C'mon girlfriend."

Tuff and Sadie stopped by their rooms above the Happy Days, packed their clothes and hurried downstairs. As they came out on to the veranda, they stopped.

"Look, Tuff, it's the little singing cowboy poet," Sadie whispered. The small cowboy sat rocking in a chair, his feet propped up on the rail and his hat back on his head, as he sang:

June's thunder booming
In Hoosier Indiana

Danger is looming
Behind the red bandana

The mean Reno boys
A Brotherhood of Outlaws
Steal everyone's toys
With smiles and cruel ha-ha's

But they soon find out
Their wicked ways are blocked
A clever giant's watch
Puts them down to sleep tick-tock

"Hey, cowboy," Tuff said. But the little elf disappeared. "He never sticks around for long. Let's go, Sadie." They ran into the stables.

"C'mon Tuff," Silver Heels neighed. "Hooter flew down and told us we're on our way to help Charlie. I can't wait to see his horse Colonel Clop again."

"Me, too. He's my favorite colt," whinnied Jenny happily.

Tuff and Sadie loaded their saddlebags, mounted up and rode out the back of the stables and up the secret trail toward The Cave. It was hidden behind Boiling Springs, a few minutes ride from Muleshoe.

Spiky, the fierce saguaro cactus, guarded the entrance to The Cave.

"Hi Tuff. Hi Sadie," Spiky said as they rode up. "Having a nice day? Did Wild Thing eat a couple of skinks?"

"Yes, she did," Sadie said. "A couple of thousand, I reckon."

"Ha," Spiky said. "Maybe that will keep her quiet for a while. Judge June told me you're going to Indiana. What's the password?"

"Doom."

"Enter and I'll send you on your way."

Tuff and Sadie rode into The Cave. It was pitch black and not a sound could be heard.

"Anyone see us?" Tuff whispered.

"No," Sadie said. "Ready."

"Alright then," said Tuff, "let's go."

Tuff and Sadie closed their eyes as a low rumble came through The Cave. They felt a cool breeze.

The rumble changed into the distant sound of thunder. They slowly walked their horses from The Cave. Black storm clouds gathered in the sky above. Tuff and Sadie rode out into soggy fields of rotten corn stalks. The air smelled of old burned wood. Just ahead, a sign said:

WELCUM TO
HOOSIER, INDIANA

If yor lookin for the
RENO GANG they were
raised here but they ain't
here anymore. They're in
their HIDEAWAY in the hills

SO SCRAM!!
SIGNED:
Brotherhood of Outlaws

Tuff spurred Silver Heels ahead. "It's very quiet," he said to Sadie as they slowly rode into Hoosier. "This town is spooky."

No sound could be heard in the little town. All of the buildings were black from fire and smoke. Bullet holes

HOTEL

HOOSIER

marked the walls. Many windows were broken. Not a person was in sight.

"It sure is," Sadie said.

"There's the rail station," Tuff said. The horses stepped carefully over the railroad tracks as they headed down  the main street.

"There must be a saloon," Sadie said. "Look, there it is."

"And there's Colonel Clop tethered in front of it," Jenny neighed.

Colonel Clop whinnied, "Good to see you fellas."

"So nice to see you too," whinnied Silver Heels.

Tuff and Sadie tied up their horses next to Colonel Clop. The sign above the saloon doors read "TEMPLE OF DOOM SALOON".

"Not a very friendly name," Tuff said. "Let's go in. Keep your bullwhip handy."

Tuff pushed the batwing doors open. As they walked into the dark room, "CRACK!" a sudden bolt of lightning struck the town, followed by the loud "BOOM!" of thunder. Sheets of rain pelted down from the stormy sky. Tuff and Sadie almost flew out of their boots. "Man, that lightning bolt was close," said Tuff.

They saw no one in the saloon. The smell of old garbage filled the room.

A throat cleared. "Welcome to Hoosier. What'll it be strangers?" said a voice from behind the bar.

"We'll have a sarsaparilla, please," Sadie said.

"Who's that?" Tuff asked as they walked up to the blond bartender.

"Here you go," said Charlie "Sir" Ringo with a smile as he put two glasses of sarsaparilla in front of them. "Man, am I glad to see you two."

CHAPTER FOUR

CHARLIE'S DISGUISE

"Geez Charlie, It's good to see you again but what an awful place," Tuff said. "This is the spookiest town we've been to in a long time. By the way, congratulations on your new job – cowboy detective."

"CRACK!" "BOOM!" Thunder rocked the saloon.

"Thanks. I'm excited but a little nervous," said Charlie. "Look, we need to be very careful. Hooter brought a spell from Judge June for me. He also helped with my disguise as a bartender. It's how I found The Reno Gang. I rode into town and said I was looking for work. They didn't know I was really looking for them."

"That's what most detectives do, isn't it?" Tuff asked. "Disguise themselves to get close to the outlaws so they learn all about their crime. Then they call in the sheriff to arrest the criminals. That's why Judge June sent us here."

"Exactly Tuff," Charlie answered. "But the outlaws know that's how we work so they're suspicious of everybody. They asked me lots of questions."

"But you don't look like a detective," Sadie said. "You look just like a cowboy."

"That's right," Charlie said. "Even when I pretend to be a bartender, I always dress as a cowboy. I even smell like one. I haven't had a bath in fifty-six days."

"Phew," Sadie said as she scrunched up her nose. "I guess they must have thought no detective would smell like that."

"What have you learned so far, Charlie?" asked Tuff.

"The 'Brotherhood of Outlaws' plan their crimes here in the saloon. A few hours ago I heard them decide to rob a train in Rockland, the nearest town. I bet they'll be back any minute with their loot."

"So you'll have evidence of a crime," Tuff said.

"Right. Then we've got two problems to solve," Charlie said. "First, John Reno is always surrounded by his brothers. They're mean and nasty and armed to protect him. To arrest John, we have to figure out a way to get him away from them."

"And the second problem?"

"If you can somehow arrest John Reno, we have to get him out of Indiana as soon as possible. The people of Indiana want to capture him and then punish him themselves. It's strange to say but we have to guard a deadly and vicious outlaw until we get him to a safe jail, where he can be brought to justice."

"We can handle the second problem," Tuff said. "Sadie and I are a sheriff and a deputy. The people will know we're on the right side of the law. But I'm not sure what to do about your first problem."

"BAM!"

The batwing doors to the saloon flew open. The floor shook as a gigantic cowboy walked into the bar.

"Remember me, Charlie?" the giant said in a surprisingly small voice. "Maybe I can help."

"Well, color me green and call me a pickle," Charlie said with a smile. "It's Gigante."

"Hello Tuff, hi Sadie," Gigante said. "I thought you might be here. I saw Silver Heels and Jenny outside. They're nuzzled up with Colonel Clop."

"What are you doing here, Gigante?" Tuff asked. "Last time we saw you you had left Macho Nacho's gang and were going to join your family in Fort Worth. We're so pleased you came on the right side of the law."

"That's right, Tuff. I heard that Charlie had joined Pinkerton as a detective. I decided that detective life sounded good for me too. Who's better to capture outlaws than a former outlaw? So I also joined Pinkerton. They asked me to be Charlie's sidekick and sent me here. I hope I got here in time to help." Gigante pulled out a beautiful gold pocket watch and checked the time.

"You bet you're in time. I'd love for you to be my sidekick," Charlie exclaimed. "Do you still drink cactus juice?"

"Yep," said Gigante. "I'll have a glass. Extra big please. Now, where are those outlaws?"

"They'll be here soon," Charlie said. "I sure like your watch."

Gigante held it up. The ticking watch

had a big white face and shiny black hands.

"Thanks Charlie. I want to show it to the outlaws and tell them 'Time's up, fellas. Gigante's in town.'"

CHAPTER FIVE

THE RENO GANG

"Did you ride one of your Spanish mares up here to Indiana, Gigante?" Charlie asked.

"I did. She's tied up just outside. Her name is Margarita."

Charlie said, "Let's get right to work. The Renos will be back soon. Gigante, you stay with me for a few minutes and we'll make a plan. Tuff, can you and Sadie hide Silver Heels and Jenny behind the saloon? Leave Colonel Clop where he is. Oh and hide your badges and hats. Then come back in."

Tuff and Sadie walked outside, took off their badges and hats and put them in their saddlebags. Then they hid their horses in a burnt-out stable behind the saloon. When they returned to the front of the saloon, they saw Gigante lead Margarita across the road and disappear behind a building.

Tuff and Sadie went back into the Temple of Doom Saloon. Charlie had set up a table and laid out a game of faro.

"Faro is the most popular card game in the Wild West," Charlie said. "John Reno hates it but the other Reno brothers love to play. In the game, you try to win each other's money. You guys sit here and start a game of faro. When the gang comes in they'll be full of cash. They'll see you and want to jump in and play the game with you."

"So if we can get all John's brothers in a game then they won't be watching him. John Reno will get bored and wander off on his own," Sadie said. "But how are we going to break away from the game and arrest him?"

"You won't arrest him yet," Charlie said. He stared toward the saloon entrance. "Gigante and I have a good plan. For now pretend you're passing through Hoosier." Charlie looked out above the batwing doors. "Here they come."

The sound of thundering hooves shook the doors of the saloon. Shouts and whistles followed.

"BAM!"

The doors flew open and four of the meanest, filthiest, nastiest bandits Tuff had ever seen barged into the saloon.

"Alright boys," John Reno hollered. "We got lucky on that train. A whole lotta rich passengers. I betcha we got thousands. Count the money, Frank. Tell me how rich I am now."

Frank Reno dumped burlap sacks full of watches, necklaces and cash on a table.

"We musta got about ten thousand worth of jewelry and cash, John."

"Hey, lookee here," William Reno snarled as he walked over to Tuff and Sadie's table. "We got us some visitors in town.

They're playin' our favorite game too. Come
on over, boys. Let's help ourselves to the game
and win these kids' money."

Frank, William and Simon Reno came
over and took seats at the faro
table. "Deal us in, boy,"

Frank said as he looked at Tuff. "What's yore name? You, too, ponytails; you got a name? Aren't you a little young to be playin' a grown-up game?"

"My name's Tuff. I don't know her name. She just rode in."

"My name's Sadie. That'll be Miss Sadie to you. And you boys better treat me with respect or I'll slap you right out of here," Sadie said as she glared at the outlaws with her fierce black eyes.

"Woohoo, we got us a sassy one," Simon Reno said. "Hey bartender, serve us up a round of red hot chili pepper juice. We need it to cool us off."

"Coming right up," Charlie said.

A loud train whistle jolted the saloon.

"WOO! WOO!"

"That must be the two o'clock train. It goes to Rockland then on to St. Louis. Should we rob it?" Frank Reno asked.

"Naw, you know we don't rob nothin' in

our home town," John Reno said as he took off his six-shooters and laid them on the bar. "But I will go out and see if our cousin Jesse's on the train. He said he might be comin' for a visit."

Tuff watched John walk out of the saloon and soon heard the whistle of the train as it left. He dealt out the cards and the Reno brothers cheated and fought among themselves as they played.

After a few deals and more arguments, Frank stood up. "Hey, where's that brother of ours?" he said. He pushed back his chair and walked out the saloon doors.

He soon burst back in, out of breath. "William, Simon, come quick! John ain't here. He disappeared."

CHAPTER SIX

JOHN RENO IS KIDNAPPED

The Reno brothers ran out onto the saloon veranda, followed by Tuff, Sadie and Charlie.

The veranda was empty. No one could be seen in the town.

What the –? thought Tuff. *It's like he disappeared into the air.*

Frank Reno whirled around, snapped out his six-shooters and pointed them at Tuff.

"Our brother ain't here," he growled. "And the only difference in this town since we came back is you and this black-haired girl." Frank turned toward Charlie. "When did these two show up? What do you know about 'em?"

"They rode in a little while after you left for Rockland, one after the other," Charlie said. "I don't know where they came from. Never seen them before."

"Where are your horses?" Frank Reno demanded.

"They're around back," Tuff answered. "We put them in the stables to get them out of the thunderstorm."

"Go back there and check, Simon," Frank Reno ordered his brother.

Simon returned after a few minutes. Tuff's heart sank when he saw what Simon had in his hands.

"Lookee here what I found," he said with a sneer. "These were in the horses' saddlebags."

He was holding Tuff and Sadie's white hats and badges.

Frank Reno glared at Tuff.

"CLICK!" went his pistol.

"Get back in the Temple of Doom, Sheriff," he said.

They walked back inside the saloon.

Tuff winced as William Reno sat he and Sadie down and tied their hands behind their chairs.

"It's time for the truth," Frank Reno said as his bloodshot eyes stared at Tuff. "Talk."

"I'm Sheriff Tuff Brunson. This is my Deputy Sadie Marcus. We're traveling from Muleshoe, Texas to Indiana. Our boss, Judge June Beak, sent us on a job to collect an outlaw. We stopped in Hoosier for a drink and a game of faro. Our horses needed a rest."

"You're lyin'," Frank Reno said. "Don't you think so, Charlie?"

"I don't know, Frank," Charlie answered. "Maybe they're telling the truth. Who are you after, Sheriff? What's the outlaw's name?"

"I can't say his name," said Tuff. "All I can tell you is the outlaw is not here in Hoosier.

You boys have got nothing to be worried about."

"Good," Frank Reno said, as he lowered his pistol. "Relax boys. Maybe this sheriff can come in handy."

"Yeah, maybe we can get him to stop a train for us so we can rob it." William grinned.

"Let's leave these two tied up," Frank Reno said to his brothers as he tightened the ropes tying Tuff and Sadie to their chairs. "We've got to find John."

"WOO! WOO!"

Tuff heard the whistle of another steam train approaching. "That's the four o'clock train from Rockland," Charlie said.

The hissing engine stopped just outside the Temple of Doom Saloon.

"BAM!" the batwing doors slammed open and a filthy cowboy in a black hat and red bandana stumbled into the saloon. Just before he collapsed on the floor, he whispered, "Which one of you is Frank Reno? Come here."

Tuff watched as Frank ran over and crouched down next to the injured cowboy.

"Frank Reno?"

"Yeah, what is it? Talk to me."

"Brother of John Reno?"

"Yes. Talk!"

"I saw your brother. He's been kidnapped. He's back in Rockland. He's the prisoner of a fierce giant named Gigante. He fears no one. He told me to tell you that if you want your brother back, bring all the money you have and meet him in Rockland in one hour. Or else."

"Gigante. The Texas outlaw," Frank Reno said to his brothers. "Is he real? I just heard rumors about him. I thought he was a myth. Oh no."

He's no myth, Tuff thought. *He's real. As you're about to find out.*

CHAPTER SEVEN

THE HUNT FOR JOHN RENO

Frank turned around and said to his brothers, "C'mon boys, we gotta go get John. Gather up some of our stolen jewelry and cash. But leave most of it here. That giant's gonna learn not to mess with the 'Brotherhood of Outlaws.' Grab our Winchester rifles and plenty of ammo."

"We'll be back soon with our brother," Simon hollered to Charlie as they galloped out of Hoosier. "Get the chili pepper juice cooled and ready."

After the gang rode off Sadie turned to Tuff and said, "Nice one, Tuff. I loved that you told the truth. 'The outlaw is not here in Hoosier.' That gang is a bunch of idiots. Of course the outlaw is not in Hoosier. He's their brother, John."

"Outlaws are never as clever as they think, Sadie." Tuff smiled. "And thanks for playing along, Charlie, pretending that you'd never seen us before."

"Like I said, they trust me," Charlie said. He untied Sadie and Tuff's hands and tied up the injured cowboy on the floor. "They have no idea I'm a detective. But we need to get going. I think Gigante has John Reno captive on the train to St. Louis. It should be stopped in Rockland. Let's get over there and help him spring a trap. We'll catch all of these bandits."

Tuff and Sadie grabbed their hats and

badges, ran to the stables and jumped up on Jenny and Silver Heels. Charlie hopped on Colonel Clop. Grabbing the reins, they rode out of Hoosier.

"Our horses are way faster than The Reno Gang's," shouted Charlie as Silver Heels, Jenny and Colonel Clop fairly flew down the muddy road. "I'll take us across the shorter back way to Rockland."

They galloped across muddy fields filled with scurrying prairie dogs and furry rabbits. Before long the town of Rockland came into view. A steam train with a locomotive pulling three cars sat idle in front of the station. The passenger car was in front, followed by the freight car in the middle then the stables car at the rear.

"Gigante said he would be in the freight car," Charlie said. "I hope he grabbed John Reno and tied him up. Gigante was to tell the train engineer and passengers to wait till we got here. They should be terrified of him and will do as he says until we take over. Let's load the horses in the stables car at the end of the train."

Charlie led the way as they hurried to the train. They walked their horses up the ramp into the stables car.

Gigante's horse Margarita whinnied, "Hello guys. It's more fun to ride the train than to carry the giant."

Tuff, Sadie and Charlie left the stables car and moved onto the freight car. Gigante was looking out the only window and smiled. "All going to plan," he said. "Here's the prisoner." John Reno was sitting on

the floor with his back against the side of the car. His hands were cuffed. He was sound asleep.

"How did you get him to fall asleep?" asked Sadie.

"I persuaded him," Gigante said with a smile. "He looked at my watch and decided it was time for bed."

"We need to get ready," said Tuff. "John's brothers are on their way here. They're bringing some cash and jewelry and think you're going to give him up if they pay it over to you."

"Ha." Gigante laughed. "They think so, huh?"

"They've got lots of pistols, rifles and ammo," Sadie added. "Enough to fight a big battle."

"Not a shot will be fired," Charlie said. "Listen to our plan. It's worked so far."

Charlie whispered the plan to Tuff and Sadie.

"Excellent idea," Tuff said. "I can see why

Pinkerton thought you and Gigante would make a great detective team."

"Let's hope it works," Charlie said. "Quick Tuff, run up to the engineer and tell him to get this train started toward St. Louis. You can stay up there with him but keep yourself hidden. The gang will try to halt the train to see if John's on board. When they do, tell the engineer to stop and invite the gang to have a look in the passenger car."

"What should I do?" Sadie asked.

"Sadie, you get in the front car and hide with the other passengers. The Reno Gang will come in looking for John Reno and won't find him. The next spot they'll check is back here in the freight car."

Tuff looked at Charlie and said, "With any luck, the gang will run in here. They'll be in for a little surprise."

"You're right, Tuff," Charlie agreed. "Let's get to work, Gigante. We don't have much time to get ready for our visitors."

CHAPTER EIGHT

NIGHTY NIGHT, OUTLAWS

Tuff hurried up to the front of the train and climbed into the engineer's compartment. The friendly engineer pulled the lever and the giant steam engine roared to life.

"Hi Sheriff," he said. "Where would you like to go?"

"Let's take the tracks toward St. Louis," Tuff said.

The train slowly started down the tracks. Tuff crouched down behind the engineer but was able to see ahead as they picked up steam.

Just after they left Rockland, the engineer slammed on the brakes and the train screeched to a halt. A giant tree trunk lay across the track.

Standing on the trunk, with their Colt 45s out and pointed at the engineer, were the three Reno brothers.

Charlie was right, Tuff thought. *The gang didn't let us get very far.*

The engineer left the brake in place and hopped down from the engine.

"Glad you were able to stop in time," said Frank Reno. "Why were you leavin' Rockland in such a hurry? Where are you goin'?"

"You boys know it's against the law to stop a train. Please move the trunk so we can pass," the engineer said. "We're late to get to St. Louis."

"Oh, we will," said William Reno. "We'd just like to have a little look around. We think our brother might be one of your passengers. He's got no reason to go to St. Louis."

"Go on then, have a look," said the engineer.

The three brothers walked back and opened the door to the passenger car. Tuff quickly climbed out the back of the engine and looked through a small window in the front of the car.

"Everybody reach for the sky," Frank Reno ordered as he waved his pistol above his head. "We ain't after your money. We're lookin' for somebody."

Tuff saw Sadie duck behind one of the other passengers as the brothers marched through the long rows of seats.

"He's not in here," Simon Reno said. "Let's look in the freight car."

As the outlaws moved out of the passenger car, Tuff hurried down to Sadie's seat. They watched as the outlaws opened the freight car door.

"They're going in," he whispered to Sadie. "I hope Charlie's ready."

The Brotherhood of Outlaws stopped in their tracks. Just inside the entrance to the car, Gigante held out his huge right arm. Dangling from his hand was a long golden chain. At the end of the chain, swinging back and forth, was the golden watch with the white face.

"Keep your eyes on the face of the watch," Gigante ordered in a steady, cool voice. "Watch it go back and forth...back and forth...back and forth...tick-tock tick-tock. Don't watch anything else. You will do as I say...you will do as I say...back and forth...back and forth...now lower your hands."

Tuff saw the three brothers stare at the watch and very slowly lower their arms. Their pistols hung limply from their hands.

"Slowly give your pistols to Charlie...give your rifles to Charlie..." Gigante whispered.

Frank, William and Simon Reno handed their Colts and Winchester rifles to Charlie. "Thanks, fellas," said Charlie as he grinned at Gigante.

"Now look into my eyes," Gigante commanded. "Look into my eyes. Now fall asleep... go to sleep..."

Gigante helped the three Renos meekly lay down on the floor of the freight car. The fearsome outlaws curled their legs up and rested their heads on their black hats. "They look like little two-year-olds at the nursery school laying down for their naps," whispered Sadie. "Maybe we should get some milk bottles warmed up for them to suck on."

"Nighty night, outlaws," Gigante whispered as he put his gold chain and watch in his pocket. "Sleep until I wake you."

"Nice work," Charlie said with a smile. "You're an excellent hypnotist."

"Great job, Gigante," Tuff said as he and Sadie joined Charlie in the freight car. "Let's get these three bandits in handcuffs. Looks like the 'Brotherhood of Outlaws' is now a 'Brotherhood of Sleeping Prisoners.'"

"Thanks, Tuff," said Gigante. The gentle giant joined Tuff as they jumped down out of the freight car. "Let's move that tree trunk."

As they passed the passenger car, one of the passengers jumped down and ran back into the town of Rockland.

I wonder where he's going? Tuff thought.

Gigante picked up the tree trunk like it was a toothpick and hurled it away from the tracks.

The engineer fired up the engine.

"Let's head to St. Louis," Tuff called to the engineer as he and Gigante climbed into the freight car. "Time to deliver this gang to the United States Federal Penitentiary."

CHAPTER NINE

GANG OF CITIZENS

The steam train picked up speed and chugged down the tracks toward St. Louis. A great cloud of white smoke trailed behind the train. Tuff and Gigante helped Sadie and Charlie line up the four sleeping Renos after locking their pistols, rifles and ammo in the freight car lockbox.

"These guys should sleep all the way to St. Louis," Charlie said as he checked their handcuffs to make sure they were tight.

"Anybody for a sarsaparilla? I've got some in my canteen."

"I'll have some," said Sadie. "Wait, look out."

Charlie's canteen smashed against the floor as the train's brakes squealed and the cars stopped.

Tuff said, "What's happening? Charlie, you and Gigante watch the prisoners. Sadie, come with me."

"OK Tuff," Sadie said.

"Oh dear," Tuff said as they hopped down off the train. "Stay close."

A group of riders on horseback surrounded the train. They wore bright red masks that covered their faces and heads, with openings for their eyes and mouths cut in the cloth. Some riders had rifles. Several had pitchforks and long knives.

Tuff tipped his hat back on his head and straightened his sheriff's star. "Keep your hand near your whip," he said to Sadie.

"Already there," she answered.

As he looked around at the silent riders, Tuff recognized the passenger who had jumped from the train. He had taken off his mask and rode in front of the others. In his hands was a long Winchester rifle.

"Sheriff," the passenger said, "I see your star. I know you have a job to do. But The Reno Gang has harmed us for many years. They've stolen, robbed and hurt the honest citizens of Indiana. Most of the time, they were arrested. Every time they escaped and carried on their outlaw ways."

So that's why he jumped off the train, Tuff thought. *This is a citizen gang. He knew we had the Renos as our prisoners.*

"I understand," Tuff said.

"Turn them over to us," the passenger said. "They will get the punishment they deserve from the citizens."

A man with him shouted, "We can throw them in the river."

Another yelled, "We'll steal everything back from their house."

A third said, "Not only that we'll take their house and horses too."

A fourth said, "And tie them to the whipping post."

"A hundred lashes each," another said.

"No, a thousand," one shouted.

"Enough," Tuff ordered. "You want revenge."

"That's right, Sheriff, we want revenge. What's so bad about that?"

"The law says these outlaws have to be tried before a judge in a court of law, where they can be sentenced for their crimes. You citizens have many ideas about how to punish them but the law only has one. That's the reason we are taking them to a prison near St. Louis. No one can escape from there. The US Army guards it."

The passenger raised his rifle to his shoulder and pointed it at Tuff.

"Sheriff, either you turn over those prisoners or you've got a gun battle on your hands," the passenger said.

"By pointing your gun at me you've just become an outlaw," Tuff said, fingering his bullwhip. "I don't take kindly to outlaws."

"CRACK!"

"Look out you dirty outlaw, here comes Sheriff Tuff Brunson."

"CRACK!"

"Here comes Deputy Sadie Marcus."

Before the passenger and his gang of citizens could move, Tuff and Sadie's whips had captured every rifle, pistol, knife and pitchfork. They sat in a pile next to the engine.

Thank you, Judge June, Tuff thought. *The spell worked again. I never thought we could take all those weapons away that fast.*

"How did you do that?" the passenger said. "Kids can't be that fast with a whip. It's magical."

Tuff answered, "Do you now understand

that we aren't turning The Reno Gang over to you? Crime doesn't pay. These outlaws will get justice from the government of the United States. I forgive you for pointing your gun at me but get on out of here and go back to your farms and towns. You can live safe from the Renos from now on."

The riders quickly turned on their horses and fled.

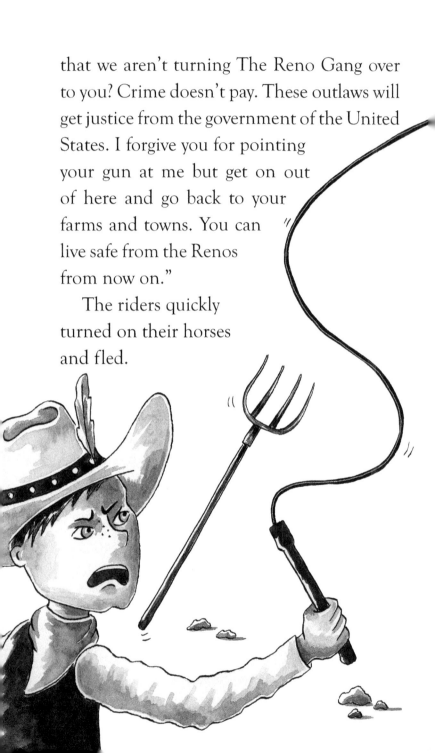

The passengers on the train cheered. The engineer pulled the train's mighty whistle, "WOO! WOO!" as the wheels began to turn.

Tuff and Sadie climbed back aboard the train where Charlie and Gigante were waiting for them.

"Well done," Charlie said.

"I've said it before and I'll say it again," said Gigante as he bowed toward Tuff and Sadie. "There is no one in the world faster with their whips than you two. You're magical."

"Next stop St. Louis," Sadie said as she winked at Tuff.

CHAPTER TEN

A HIDEOUT KIDS REUNION

The train chugged along and was soon in St. Louis. A platoon of soldiers waited at the station.

"OK boys, time to get up," Gigante said to the Reno brothers. He nudged them awake. "We've got a nice group of soldiers who will look after you. Now run along with them."

John Reno and his brothers stood up. They raised their cuffed hands and rubbed sleep out of their eyes. The soldiers helped them down from the freight car into a waiting prison wagon.

A sign above the iron door on the wagon said:

THE WAY OF THE SCOFFLAW
IS HARD
ADMISSION: 1 DOLLAR

"Don't worry, boys," Tuff said. "You don't have to pay admission to the prison. You get in for free."

Charlie, Gigante and Sadie all laughed as they opened the stables car. They led their horses down the ramp into the bright sunshine.

"Feels good to stretch our legs," Margarita neighed.

"Let's get back to Spiky," Silver Heels whinnied. "I know the way."

"Come with us, Charlie. Judge June wants to speak with you about your new job as a cowboy detective," Tuff said. "You too, Gigante."

Silver Heels led the way as the four horses breezed through a nearby cornfield. The fierce cactus Spiky soon appeared out of nowhere. Behind Spiky was The Cave entrance.

"Howdy Tuff, howdy Sadie, howdy Charlie. Whoa, who's the big guy? We haven't met," Spiky said as he stared into Gigante's eyes. "You're as tall as I am."

"My name's Gigante," the giant said politely. "I'm Charlie's sidekick. Nice to meet you. I'd shake hands but I've never shaken hands with a cactus before. It might sting."

"Is he coming with you back to Muleshoe, Tuff? Judge June didn't say anything about him," Spiky said, ignoring Gigante.

"He is," Tuff said. "Judge June wants to meet him. She told us before we left."

"Why are we going in this cave, Tuff?" Gigante asked, trembling. "I'm afraid of caves."

"You'll be fine, shorty," Spiky said. "Tuff, you know I don't like surprises but I'll let the little guy in. What's the password?"

"Doom."

"Enter."

Tuff, Sadie, Charlie and Gigante rode into The Cave. It was pitch black and not a sound could be heard.

"Anyone see us?" Tuff whispered.

"No," Sadie said. "Ready."

"Alright then," said Tuff. "Let's go."

They closed their eyes as a low rumble came through The Cave. They felt a cool breeze.

Bright sunshine greeted them as they rode out. Huge yellow monarch butterflies fluttered around the sparkling green trees. The scent

of peanut-butter cupcakes surrounded The Cave's entrance.

"Hello and welcome back," Judge June said with a smile as she rode up on her horse, Rowdy.

Behind Judge June, on a beautiful dappled gray horse with a long white muzzle, was a girl. She looked like Sadie, with black hair and ponytails. Unlike Sadie, her ponytails were braided with bright colored red, gold and blue ribbons.

"Who's that?" Sadie asked Tuff. "I haven't seen her before. Have you?"

"No," Tuff said. "But I'm sure Judge June will tell us who she is."

"Here's your golden star, Tuff," Judge June said. "Congrats on arresting The Reno Gang. Both Pinkerton and the president of the United States sent me a telegram with the news. The president is so pleased. You are invited to visit him in the White House."

"Wow," Tuff said. "Can we all go? We

worked as a team."

"Of course. Hi Sadie, well done. Good to see you again, Charlie. Great going on your first Pinkerton job. And this little fella must be Gigante," Judge June said as she stared up into the sky at the smiling giant's happy face.

"He is," Tuff said. "We invited him back with us, as you suggested. We were sure surprised to find out he's Charlie's sidekick."

"Nice to meet you, Judge June. I am honored to be here in Muleshoe," Gigante said as he bowed toward the good witch.

"Well, we are happy to have you here. From now on, you are a hideout kid. The very biggest one."

Tuff's pet, the polite beaver Mr. Zip, ran along the ground and hopped up on Tuff's lap. He looked up at Gigante and said, "Hello, sir, nice to meet you."

"Oh, I bet you're wondering who our new friend is," Judge June said. The girl behind her smiled and rode forward. "This is Miss

Hannah Humblebee. She's also a new hideout kid. Hannah's a Hopi Tribe Indian girl detective who has come to live in Muleshoe. I've asked her to work for me and help solve crimes among the Native American people. Her horse's name is Blackberry."

"That's wonderful news," Tuff said. "The Hopi Tribe is peaceful, kind and wise. Welcome, Miss Hannah."

"Hello everyone," Miss Hannah Humblebee said in a soft voice. "I'm so happy to join you and I hope to help Judge June, Tuff and Sadie bring outlaws to justice."

"Oh yeah?" Sadie said. "I'm not sure we need a lot of help."

Hannah said, "Sadie, I'm a detective, like Charlie. I solve mysteries. You arrest the outlaws. We don't have the same job. We can work together."

"She's right, Sadie," Charlie said. "Just like you worked with me to capture The Reno Gang. Welcome Hannah."

"OK," Sadie said. She stared at the ground.

"Welcome Blackberry," neighed all the horses as they bowed their heads.

"Hello," Blackberry whinnied as she nodded in return.

"Let's ride down to the Happy Days Saloon," Judge June said. "We have a lot to catch up on. I want to hear about hypnotizing outlaws."

"You bet," Gigante said. "Just don't look at my watch too closely. I might hypnotize you into giving us free sarsaparilla and s'mores."

"You'll get those anyway." Judge June laughed. "Giddy up, Rowdy."

THE END

Author's Note

Each of the Hideout Kids series of books features several of the same characters, animals, places and things. Here are some brief descriptions:

Charlie "Sir" Ringo: A cowboy detective.

Deputy Joe "Sawbones" Newton: Muleshoe's doctor, a deputy to Sheriff Tuff Brunson.

Deputy Sadie Marcus: Ten-year-old deputy of Muleshoe and Tuff's best friend.

Hooter: Judge June's familiar. An owl-shaped spirit who helps Judge June practice her magic.

Jack: Sawbones' horse.

Jelly Roll Jim, Toothless Tom, Deputy Dan Pigeon: Teenagers who grew up in Muleshoe and stayed on to help Judge June and the hideout kids.

Jenny: Sadie's horse. A gift from Chief Ten Bears of the Comanche Tribe Indians.

Judge Junia "June" Beak: United States District Judge of the West. She is also a good and powerful witch.

Mesquite trees: Typical tree of the Texas desert.

Miss Hannah Humblebee: A Hopi Tribe Indian girl detective.

Mr. Zip: Tuff's pet. A beaver.

Muleshoe, Texas: Home of the hideout kids. Only children can find it and live there.

S'mores: Chocolate-covered marshmallows, served on sugar crackers. Dee-lish.

Sarsaparilla: The most popular soft drink of the Wild West. It's thought to have healing powers and is made from the root of the sarsaparilla vine. Yummy.

Sheriff Tuff Brunson: Ten-year-old sheriff of Muleshoe.

Silver Heels: Tuff's horse. Also a gift from Chief Ten Bears.

Spiky: A giant saguaro cactus that guards The Cave.

The Cave: A magical place where the kids can travel through time.

The Singing Cowboy Poet: A magical elf.

Wild Thing: Judge June's pet. A pink fairy armadillo.

Here are descriptions of a few animals, plants, people and things that you might not have heard of before and which appear in this book:

Bartender: The person who serves drinks and food at a saloon.

Cicada: Insects that make a loud drumming sound using their tummies.

Colt 45: The most popular pistol in the Wild West.

Engineer: The person in charge of driving a train.

Fez of armadillos: A group of armadillos is known as a "fez".

Pinkerton: The first private detective agency set up in the nineteenth century in America.

Prairie dogs: They are not dogs at all; they are rodents, like rats. In the days of the Wild West they were the most common mammals to be found in America.

Ringleader: The leader of a group.

Saguaro cactus: A large cactus, covered in spikes, commonly found in the southwestern part of America.

Scofflaw: Another word for outlaw.

Skink: A member of the lizard family. When attacked, its tail will fall off and continue to wiggle on the ground, hopefully distracting whatever is attacking it.

Winchester rifle: The most popular rifle in the Wild West.

DETECTIVE HANNAH HUMBLEBEE: THE CASE OF BLUE DUCK & BELLE STARR

Chapter One

WILD THING HAS A BATH

A bright autumn sun was high in the sky above the Wild West Texas town of Muleshoe. It was lunchtime on Halloween Eve. Detective Miss Hannah Humblebee closed the book she was reading – *Mystery Crimes of the Old West* – and placed it on the bookshelf above her desk. *I can't wait to see who did it*, she thought. *I bet the rattlesnakes are involved. I wonder what's for lunch?*

Hannah walked out the door of her one-room detective's office. The sign above the door read *Miss Hannah Humblebee, Detective: The Detective is IN*. She changed the *IN* to *OUT*, walked across Main Street and joined the other hideout kids gathered in the Happy Days Saloon. A big bowl of spicy pumpkin soup steamed from the center of the round main table.

Just after Hannah walked in, ten-year-olds Sheriff Tuff Brunson and Deputy Sadie Marcus strolled into the Happy Days.

"Hi Tuff. Hi Sadie," Hannah said. "Happy Halloween Eve. Doesn't the soup smell delicious?"

"Hello, Miss Hannah," Tuff said.

"I hate pumpkin soup," Sadie said as she glared at the steaming bowl. "Why did Jelly Roll Jim put pumpkins in the soup? It's silly to eat a jack o'lantern. Why can't we just have chicken noodle soup?" She grabbed Jelly Roll Jim's beautiful silver serving spoon and hid it in her rucksack.

"Sadie," Tuff scolded, "put that back. And guess what? Hannah just said hi to you."

Sadie put that spoon in her bag, Hannah thought. *Probably she'll say she "borrowed" it.*

"Phew, what's that smell? It's worse than rotten pumpkins," Sadie said, ignoring both Tuff and Hannah.

"I can solve that puzzle. That's the smell of a pink fairy armadillo who's never had a bath," Hannah said.

"Who'd like a bowl of mash?" Wild Thing, Judge June's pet pink fairy armadillo, growled as she popped out from under the table. "Oh wait, you can't. I'm the only one who gets to eat mash. Where's my bowl, Jelly Roll Jim? Gimme. Gimme now."

"You're right about the cause of the smell, Hannah," Tuff said.

"Here you go, sweetheart," said Jelly Roll Jim to Wild Thing. "A nice big bowl of smushed centipedes and earwigs. Hey, what are those spots all over you?"

"That's my Halloween costume. I'm pretending to have chicken pox."

The Muleshoe doctor, Joe "Sawbones" Newton, ran into the saloon. "Anybody seen that rascal Wild Thing?" he asked. "She's got chicken pox. She's highly contagious. We all need to stay away from her. Wait, I can smell her. She's here."

"Chicken pox? Oh, no," Tuff, Sadie and the children cried as they fled the saloon. Hannah looked at Sawbones then at Wild Thing's spots and thought, *Those don't look real to me. Someone's playing a trick on Wild Thing.*

"Come back," said Wild Thing. "Now nobody will play with me. Boo hoo."

Hannah turned to the door and said, "Look, here comes Mr. Zip. I bet he'll play with you."

Mr. Zip, Tuff's pet beaver, walked through the doors. "Why did everybody just run away?" he asked.

"Cause I've got chicken pox," Wild Thing said. "I don't know how. I never hang out with chickens. I hate 'em. I told the kids I was pretending to have the pox but Sawbones told them I really have it. He's always getting in the way of my fun."

"You shouldn't have lied to the kids," Mr. Zip scolded. "I've never had it but I know that chicken pox is contagious. Nobody wants to spend Halloween scratching a bunch of bumps on their skin. Come with me. I've got a way to get rid of that pox."

Hmm, Hannah thought. *Mr. Zip said that chicken pox is contagious but he's happy to be with Wild Thing. So he's not afraid of catching it from her. Something's odd about that. I bet she doesn't really have the pox.*

"Oh, yeah mister goody four paws?" said Wild Thing. "If you can fix me I might actually like you for five minutes."

Hannah watched Mr. Zip lead Wild Thing away from the saloon. She noticed Sawbones giggling. "I know why you're laughing," she said. "You figured out a way to get that armadillo in the water. I bet you painted those spots on her."

"That's right. Wild Thing fell for our trick," said Sawbones. "While she was asleep the kids and I used a bucket of cactus juice to paint spots on her. Now Mr. Zip will give her a treat."

"I knew it. That's why Mr. Zip isn't afraid of catching chicken pox. That's very naughty, Sawbones. But I've got to see this," Hannah said. "Let's follow them and watch." They stepped out of the Happy Days and followed the two pets.

"C'mon, Wild Thing," said Mr. Zip. "I've dammed up the stream and made a nice pond. I mixed a special medicine in the water. All you have to do is jump in and the chicken pox will be cured."

"But I hate water," said Wild Thing as they neared the pond. "I never have a bath.

I never jump in ponds. No, no, no."

"Just walk up and smell the pond," Mr. Zip said. "Get your nose really close. You'll like the smell. It smells like dead eels, snakes and lizards."

Wild Thing crawled up and stuck her snout above the pond water. "That does smell yummy."

Sadie whispered to Hannah and Tuff, "Now this will be funny."

Mr. Zip crept forward, whipped his big flat paddle tail around and "SLAP!" knocked Wild Thing on her bottom. She flew out into the middle of the pond.

"SPLASH!"

"You meany beaver." Wild Thing yelped and thrashed around in the pond.

"Ha, ha, ha." The hideout kids roared with laughter when they saw the pink fairy armadillo splash and holler as she made her way to the bank.

"You fell for our trick, now you had your

treat. We finally got you to take a bath. First time in your life," Not-So-Fast Freddie said.

"See, look, the spots are gone," Mr. Zip said.

"I'll get you back." Wild Thing shook off the water and snarled. "Every one of you."

"Oh dear," Judge Junia "June" Beak said as she appeared by the side of the pond. "Did you have a little swim, Wild Thing? I thought you hated water."

"Grr. Grr," said Wild Thing.

Judge June, the good witch who ruled over Muleshoe, turned to Hannah. "Let's go over to your office. I've got a job for you in another territory. Sadie, please join us. I'd like you to go with Hannah."

"Is there a mystery to solve?" Hannah asked.

"There could be," Judge June answered.

"Where are you sending us?"

"Oklahoma. Indian Territory."

MIKE GLEASON

HIDEOUT KIDS

TUFF, SADIE
& THE WILD WEST

MIKE GLEASON

HIDEOUT KIDS

GENERAL MUSTER
& NO-TREES TOWN

MIKE GLEASON

HIDEOUT KIDS

GRIZZLY BEARS
& BEAVER PELTS

MIKE GLEASON

HIDEOUT KIDS

MACHO NACHO
& THE COWBOY BATTLE

MIKE GLEASON

HIDEOUT KIDS

THE PARROT GANG
& WILD WEST GHOSTS

MIKE GLEASON

HIDEOUT KIDS

BILLY THE KID
& CROOKED JIM

MIKE GLEASON

HIDEOUT KIDS

JUDGE ROY BEAN
& WILD THING

MIKE GLEASON

HIDEOUT KIDS

DETECTIVE CHARLIE "SIR" RINGO
THE CASE OF THE
BROTHERHOOD
OF OUTLAWS

MR. ZIP

WILD THING

JUDGE JUNE

SPIKY

CHARLIE "SIR" RINGO

ABOUT THE AUTHOR

Hideout Kids author Mike Gleason comes from a small town in Texas. He grew up with cowboys, cowgirls and exciting stories of Wild West adventures. He was a wildcatter in the Texas oil fields and a board director at MGM in Hollywood. He created and produced an award-winning music television series at Abbey Road Studios. He lives and writes in London.

ABOUT THE ILLUSTRATOR

Hideout Kids illustrator Victoria Taylor comes from Cheltenham, England, and her love of art was inspired by her maternal grandmother. She trained at Plymouth University and worked for many years as a graphic designer. Having returned to her first love of painting and drawing, Victoria is now a freelance book illustrator. She lives in Gloucestershire with her husband and two children.

Printed in Great Britain
by Amazon

37296129R00078